Jeremy Strong once worked in a bakery, putting the jam into three thousand doughnuts every night. Now he puts the jam in stories instead, which he finds much more exciting. At the age of three, he fell out of a first-floor bedroom window and landed on his head. His mother says that this damaged him for the rest of his life and refuses to take any responsibility. He loves writing stories because he says it is 'the only time you alone have complete control and can make anything happen'. His ambition is to make you laugh (or at least snuffle). Jeremy Strong lives near Bath with his wife, Gillie, four cats and a flying cow.

Are you feeling silly enough to read more?

THE BATTLE FOR CHRISTMAS
THE BEAK SPEAKS
BEWARE! KILLER TOMATOES
CHICKEN SCHOOL
DINOSAUR POX
GIANT JIM AND THE HURRICANE
I'M TELLING YOU, THEY'RE ALIENS
THE INDOOR PIRATES
THE INDOOR PIRATES ON TREASURE ISLAND
INVASION OF THE CHRISTMAS PUDDINGS
THE KARATE PRINCESS
THE KARATE PRINCESS TO THE RESCUE
KRAZY COW SAVES THE WORLD – WELL, ALMOST
LET'S DO THE PHARAOH!
PANDEMONIUM AT SCHOOL
PIRATE PANDEMONIUM
THE SHOCKING ADVENTURES OF LIGHTNING LUCY
THERE'S A PHARAOH IN OUR BATH!
THERE'S A VIKING IN MY BED AND OTHER STORIES
TROUBLE WITH ANIMALS

Read about Streaker's adventures:
THE HUNDRED-MILE-AN-HOUR DOG
RETURN OF THE HUNDRED-MILE-AN-HOUR DOG
WANTED! THE HUNDRED-MILE-AN-HOUR DOG
LOST! THE HUNDRED-MILE-AN-HOUR DOG

Read about Nicholas's daft family:
MY DAD'S GOT AN ALLIGATOR!
MY GRANNY'S GREAT ESCAPE
MY MUM'S GOING TO EXPLODE!
MY BROTHER'S FAMOUS BOTTOM
MY BROTHER'S FAMOUS BOTTOM GETS PINCHED
MY BROTHER'S FAMOUS BOTTOM GOES CAMPING
MY BROTHER'S HOT CROSS BOTTOM

JEREMY STRONG'S LAUGH-YOUR-SOCKS-OFF
JOKE BOOK

LAUGH YOUR SOCKS OFF WITH

Jeremy STRONG

Dinosaur Pox

Illustrated by

Nick Sharratt

PUFFIN

*This is for everyone in Birmingham who made me so welcome,
especially David and Jenny and the lunch-providers!*

PUFFIN BOOKS

Published by the Penguin Group
Penguin Books Ltd, 80 Strand, London WC2R 0RL, England
Penguin Group (USA) Inc., 375 Hudson Street, New York, New York 10014, USA
Penguin Group (Canada), 90 Eglinton Avenue East, Suite 700, Toronto, Ontario, Canada M4P 2Y3
(a division of Pearson Penguin Canada Inc.)
Penguin Ireland, 25 St Stephen's Green, Dublin 2, Ireland (a division of Penguin Books Ltd)
Penguin Group (Australia), 250 Camberwell Road, Camberwell, Victoria 3124, Australia
(a division of Pearson Australia Group Pty Ltd)
Penguin Books India Pvt Ltd, 11 Community Centre, Panchsheel Park, New Delhi – 110 017, India
Penguin Group (NZ), 67 Apollo Drive, Rosedale, North Shore 0632, New Zealand
(a division of Pearson New Zealand Ltd)
Penguin Books (South Africa) (Pty) Ltd, 24 Sturdee Avenue, Rosebank, Johannesburg 2196, South Africa

Penguin Books Ltd, Registered Offices: 80 Strand, London WC2R 0RL, England

puffinbooks.com

Published in Puffin Books 1999
This edition published 2009 for The Book People Ltd,
Hall Wood Avenue, Haydock, St Helens WA11 9UL
1

Text copyright © Jeremy Strong, 1999
Illustrations copyright © Nick Sharratt, 1999
All rights reserved

The moral right of the author and illustrator has been asserted

Set in Baskerville MT
Made and printed in England by Clays Ltd, St Ives plc

British Library Cataloguing in Publication Data
A CIP catalogue record for this book is available from the British Library

ISBN: 978-0-141-32785-3

www.greenpenguin.co.uk

Penguin Books is committed to a sustainable future
for our business, our readers and our planet.
The book in your hands is made from paper
certified by the Forest Stewardship Council.

Contents

1 Jodie's Extraordinary Trick

Maybe it happened because Jodie Bolton fancied a change. Maybe it didn't, but Jodie was fed up with the way things were. If she had to write a list of the things she disliked most, it would have looked like this:

1 *Her hair* She had short, dark, curly hair and she had always hated it. When she was seven she had sneaked off with Mum's best scissors, shut herself in the bathroom and cut most of it off. This was not simply to get rid of it, but in the strange hope that when it grew back it would be long and blonde.

What Jodie wanted was long, blonde, straight hair like a fairy-tale princess. The sort of hair you could do things with like putting it into French plaits, or even a simple ponytail. Jodie thought short, dark, curly hair was useless and horrible.

2 *Freckles* There weren't just a few scattered across her nose, like some of her friends had: these freckles were EVERYWHERE. They had marched across her nose, conquered her cheeks, invaded her forehead and even colonized her ear lobes. Jodie reckoned her face looked like the car windscreen in summer – splattered all over with tiny dead flies.

3 *Her brother, Mark* She was ten and he was only nine, so how come he was already taller than she was? They got on like two scorpions shut in a box only big enough for one. (Not that it was ever Jodie's fault. She was the oldest, and full of common sense – how could it possibly be *her* fault?)

4   *She didn't like being bossed around* Jodie wished she was big and powerful enough to do all the bossing herself.

In other words, LIFE WAS UNFAIR and she frequently told her parents just how unfair it was.

'But, Jodie,' said Mr Bolton, 'life is unfair to everybody. You'll understand that as you get older.'

This comment was supposed to make Jodie feel better. It didn't. Jodie was grumpy at home, grumpy at school, grumpy at mealtimes, grumpy at bedtime and, well, just generally grumpy.

'Why don't you enjoy yourself more?' suggested Mum.

'What is there to enjoy?' muttered Jodie,

and she went stamping upstairs and looked in her bedroom mirror. *I'm sure I'm getting more freckles. I think my freckles are having baby freckles all over my face.*

Mark put his head round the door. 'You'll turn into stone,' he grinned.

'What?'

'If you stare at yourself in that mirror you'll turn into stone. Ugly, scary faces always turn people into stone.'

'Ha, very-funny-I-don't-think, ha.'

'Oh well, suit yourself. Dad says come down for tea.'

When they sat down, Mum put a vegetable lasagne on the table.

'It hasn't got any meat in it!' whined Mark.

'That's because it's a *vegetable* lasagne,' Mum explained patiently.

'Lasagne is meant to have meat in it!'

'Not if it's a vegetable lasagne,' Jodie pointed out.

Mark fixed his big sister with a threatening glare. 'It's all because you're a vegetarian. We're only having this because of *you*!'

Mr Bolton sighed quietly. 'Vegetables are good for all of us,' he said.

'So is meat,' protested Mark. 'Anyhow, what's wrong with eating meat?'

'It's wrong to kill animals,' Jodie said.

'Not if you want to eat them it isn't.

Anyhow, what about killing vegetables? Why isn't it wrong to kill vegetables?'

'Don't be stupid, Mark. You can't kill a vegetable,' Jodie snapped.

'Oh yeah? How do you know? Just because you don't hear onions yelling when you slice them up doesn't mean they don't feel anything.'

Mrs Bolton had turned a shade paler. 'Really, Mark, I think that's just a bit fanciful, you know.'

For a few moments Mark remained quiet. He was brooding on something. 'The dinosaurs were vegetarians,' he muttered darkly. 'They were herbivores. Look what happened to them.'

'What did happen to them, Mark?' his father asked politely.

'They died out. Extinct. Kaput. Gone for ever.' Mark leaned across the table and grinned at his big sister. 'You're going to become extinct.'

Mrs Bolton gave a quiet giggle while her husband frowned and wagged a finger at Jodie.

'You have been warned,' he said, in a Voice of Doom.

'This family is so amusing,' Jodie said icily, and after that things were quiet for a while.

After they had eaten, when Mr Bolton was stacking the dishwasher, he said he wished that Jodie wasn't so miserable.

'I'd just like her to be happy,' he said. 'Not all the time, but sometimes. She never seems to enjoy anything.'

'She'll grow out of it,' said Mum.

'When? How long do we have to wait?'

'Don't worry,' said Mum, little knowing what Jodie was about to do.

*

That night something unusual happened. In fact it was more than unusual – it was extraordinary, incredible, fantastic, mind-boggling and bizarre – and it happened to Jodie.

Nobody knew how it happened, or why it happened. All they knew was that when Jodie went to bed she was herself – in other words, grumpy – but when Jodie woke up the next morning she had changed. She wasn't Jodie any longer.

She was a dinosaur.

It was a dinosaur that got out of bed the next day – a dinosaur with fat, stumpy legs like thick tree trunks. Instead of freckles, she had purple and green blotches all over her fat, scaly body. She had a long thick tail. She had great leathery plates sticking out of her back, like fins that had been designed by somebody who couldn't draw. She had a

small head with little
red glinting eyes, a
long snout, and an
even longer thick
purple tongue.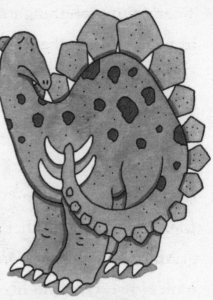

Jodie knew
something was wrong
the moment she woke
up. She struggled
across to her mirror.

'Oh, isn't that just great,' she muttered.
'I'm a dinosaur. Just my luck. Why does
nothing nice ever happen to me? First I'm
given freckles and horrible hair, and now I've
turned into a dinosaur.'

She suddenly had a thought. Maybe she
had stared at herself in the mirror too long,
just like Mark said.

Jodie trotted across to Mark's room and
pushed open his door with her snout. 'You

were wrong,' she announced triumphantly. 'I haven't turned into stone. I've turned into a dinosaur, so there.'

Mark took one look at his sister and his jaw dropped. 'Wow!' he breathed. 'That is incredible! How did you do it? Can I do it too?' He fished around in a box beneath his bed and pulled out a plastic dinosaur. 'You're just like this model. You're a stegosaurus.'

Jodie was secretly pleased that, just for once, she had managed to impress her brother, but Mr and Mrs Bolton were not impressed at all.

'How long are you going to stay like that?'

asked Dad. 'You've got school in fifteen minutes.'

'Everyone will laugh at me,' complained Jodie.

'They laugh at you anyway,' smirked Mark. 'Shall I put your cereal on the floor, or are you going to sit up at the table?'

'Don't tease,' said Mum, putting Jodie's bowl on the kitchen floor.

'I don't want it anyway,' grumbled Jodie.

'You must eat something.'

'I expect she wants plants,' said Mark. 'Stegosauruses were plant eaters.'

Jodie hated to admit it, but Mark was right. She did fancy some plants.

'It's because you're a vegetarian,' Mark claimed. 'Eating all those vegetables has turned you into a dinosaur.'

Mrs Bolton let Jodie out into the back garden and watched as her daughter wandered round the flower beds chewing bushes and nibbling at tender buds. 'Oh dear, I rather liked those big white daisies, but Jodie seems to like them too.'

When Dad left for work, he decided he ought to make an appointment for Jodie at the doctor's surgery. 'I've never heard of a child turning into a dinosaur before, but maybe the doctor has. I'm sure Jodie will be back to normal soon.'

'Jodie? Normal?' sniggered Mark. 'That's impossible.'

Dad's face clouded. He was worried that Mark was quite probably right. On the other hand, he didn't really fancy bringing up a dinosaur in the family.

2 A Bad-hair Day

Mrs Bolton sent Jodie into school with a note for her teacher.

> Dear Mrs Farouk,
>
> Jodie turned into a dinosaur last night, but she seems to be quite well in herself. My husband has made an appointment for her to see the doctor, just in case. The big bunch of flowers is her lunch. She seems to prefer daisies.
>
> Yours sincerely,
> Mrs Bolton

Mrs Farouk was not at all sure she should have a dinosaur in her class, especially one that wasn't

wearing school uniform. Jodie's clothes didn't fit any longer of course, but Mrs Bolton had managed to get a school tie round her neck, even though the tie bit was rather short.

Jodie was the centre of attention, not surprisingly. Most of the children thought it was brilliant and wished that they had thought of coming to school as a dinosaur. Rebecca Bangle was the only one who laughed.

Rebecca Bangle was generally considered to be the most beautiful girl in the school and the boys always made a fuss of her. However, a stegosaurus in the classroom was far more exciting than

14

Rebecca, and everyone flocked round Jodie, who was delighted to get so much attention for once.

'I think it's stupid,' said Rebecca, tossing back her long blonde hair. 'Why have you come to school as a dinosaur?' she demanded.

'I'll come to school however I like,' answered Jodie. 'I shall probably come as a tiger tomorrow and eat you.'

'Bet you won't – Spotty.'

'Spotty yourself.'

'I have not got spots!' yelled Rebecca, because she did have lovely clear skin.

'You have so,' Jodie retorted. 'I saw them when you were changing for swimming. You've got spots all over your fat b –'

'Girls! Girls!' interrupted Mrs Farouk hastily. 'Go to your desk, Rebecca. Now Jodie, where are you going to sit?'

'On my bottom, like everyone else,' Jodie answered, and the class burst out laughing.

'But you can't sit at your desk,' said Mrs Farouk.

'I shall sit *by* my desk,' Jodie insisted.

'But how will you write?'

'With difficulty,' Jodie admitted. 'Anyhow, it's Tuesday, and we always have PE first thing on a Tuesday.' Jodie was thinking that PE would be OK. It had always been her favourite. (She just made sure that she never told anyone she was enjoying herself.)

But before the class could have PE, they trooped into the hall for assembly. When they sang a hymn, Jodie joined in and suddenly everyone else stopped singing and listened to her, because Jodie couldn't sing like a girl any longer – she sang like a dinosaur. Her voice was as tender as sandpaper. There was no tune at all. It was more like endless grunting mixed with a squeaky snarl.

The headteacher was definitely *not* impressed. 'Jodie Bolton!' cried Miss Gatling. 'Go and stand over there by yourself. How dare you spoil our hymn.'

'I didn't do it on purpose. I was trying to sing.'

'I am not going to stand here arguing with

a stegosaurus,' snapped Miss Gatling. 'Do as you're told.'

'It's not fair,' muttered Jodie, and she went and stood in the corner. She had not been there very long before a desperate urge overcame her. She began to twitch and lift her thick legs and stamp on the floor. She whisked her tail and pressed her wrinkly knees together hard – all four of them. Miss Gatling soon noticed.

'Oh, for goodness sake! Whatever is the matter with you now?' she said at last.

'Can I go to the toilet?'

'Yes – go, go!'

Jodie pounded off to the girls' lavatory and skidded to a lumbering halt at the door.

This was ridiculous. How could a dinosaur sit on a toilet seat? She glanced around desperately. Everyone was still in the hall. Jodie slipped outside and found a nice big bush. She disappeared behind it for several seconds and when she came back she felt a lot better. The bush tasted nice too.

PE turned out to be a bit of a disaster. In the changing room Jodie stared at her PE bag, hanging on a peg.

'What's the matter?' asked Carly.

'I've got four feet and only two plimsolls,' Jodie growled, 'and there's no way I shall ever get my leotard on.'

'What about your netball skirt?'

'Don't be daft, Carly, look at the size of me. I'd need six skirts to go round this waist.'

'So – you can borrow mine, and Susanna's and Fran's and so on. We'll hook them all together to make one big skirt.'

The skirts were fed round Jodie's enormous belly until it looked as if she was wearing some kind of strange ballet frock.

'Oh look,' cried Rebecca as they lined up.
'It's the dancing dinosaur.'

'Pimple-bottom,' Jodie snapped back, and
even Mrs Farouk hid a smile.

Jodie liked climbing the ropes most of all,
but it was obvious she wouldn't be able to do
that now. Anyway, Mrs Farouk wanted her
class to practise backward rolls. Jodie, who
prided herself on her athletic skills, found that
the best she could manage was a sort of
accidental tumble sideways.

She crashed to the ground and almost
squashed poor Mrs
Farouk, who just
managed to leap out
of the way in time.
'Silly girl! Go and do
some jumps over the
box, and do try and be
more graceful.'

Jodie took a good run at the springboard. She launched herself into the air and landed on the board with an ear-splitting CCRRAA-CCKK! She watched glumly as the two halves of the broken board went spinning up into the air and clattered to the ground, sending splinters flying in all directions. Jodie stood there, surrounded by bits of broken wood.

'This really is too much, Jodie. You'll have to go back to the classroom.'

Jodie stomped off sadly. She barged around the classroom for a while, getting bored and hungry. She ate all Mrs Farouk's pot plants and then went outside to the school garden. There were plenty of delicious bushes to eat out there. She happily munched away until the garden had been reduced to a ragged mass of chewed branches and thin twigs.

At break-time, things got worse. Everyone

wanted to play with Jodie, which made a nice change, but they wanted rides on her back. Children kept trying to clamber up her sides and sit on top of her. Jodie found it very tiresome and eventually she lost her temper. She lifted her head, shook it angrily and roared.

'Raaaaaaaaargh!'

Everyone froze. They stared at Jodie. Her eyes flashed. She snorted down both nostrils, and she began to move. Her huge feet stamped on the hard ground and her body rocked backwards and forwards. And then she charged, bellowing and shaking her head wildly from side to side. Round and round the playground she went, roaring and galloping like a rhino having a major temper tantrum.

Children scattered in every direction, screaming. It was a stampede. The teacher on duty watched in astonishment as the playground emptied of children in just a few seconds.

As the children vanished Jodie slowed down and stood in the middle of the playground, panting and feeling very pleased with herself. Mr Grant, the teacher on duty, approached carefully.

'I think you had better come with me and explain yourself to Miss Gatling,' he said. But there was no need, because at that moment Miss Gatling and Mrs Farouk both came hurrying out of the building. They were wondering why the school was suddenly full of whimpering, scared children.

'What's been going on?' demanded the headteacher. Then, before Jodie or Mr Grant could answer, Miss Gatling saw the state of the school garden. 'Our lovely garden! It's ruined! Is this your doing, Jodie Bolton?'

'I was hungry,' Jodie explained.

'Hungry? You've eaten our entire garden!'

'My stomach is bigger than it used to be,' Jodie pointed out, with great logic.

Miss Gatling, however, was not the least bit sympathetic. 'You've got a lot of explaining to do, young lady. Why is the whole school in tears?'

'Jodie roared at them,' said Mr Grant.

'Roared at them? What kind of behaviour is that for a pupil at this school? What kind of roar?' enquired the headteacher, turning to Mr Grant, who shifted his feet, feeling rather embarrassed. He turned a delicate pink colour.

'Well,' he began slowly, 'it was a sort of *Rrrrrr*!'

'A sort of *Rrrrrr*! That doesn't sound too frightening,' Miss Gatling remarked. 'Did it scare you, Mrs Farouk?'

'No – not really.'

'It was louder,' Mr Grant said lamely. 'More a sort of *RRRRRRR*!!'

Miss Gatling took two steps back and clutched Mrs Farouk.

'Sorry,' muttered Mr Grant, and the three adults fixed their gaze on Jodie.

Miss Gatling took a deep breath. 'Did you roar like that at the children?'

Jodie was silent. She stared sullenly at the ground.

'Perhaps you can do it again,' said Miss Gatling icily, 'so that we may have the privilege of hearing it for ourselves.'

'I don't want to,' Jodie answered through clenched teeth.

Miss Gatling fixed her with a steely glare. 'I am trying hard to understand a very unusual event in the playground, Jodie, so please oblige me by roaring.'

Jodie coughed and cleared her throat. This was quite ridiculous. 'Rrrrrrrrr.'

Miss Gatling raised one eyebrow. 'Is that it?'

'It was louder,' Mr Grant put in, folding his arms.

'Roar again, louder.'

Jodie rolled her eyes. 'Rrrrrrr!'

'Louder!' cried Miss Gatling. 'Make it louder, girl, and don't you roll your eyes at me!'

Something deep inside Jodie snapped. This was too much. What was wrong with

everyone today? She threw back her head
and opened her mouth.

'**RRRRRRRGGGGG-
HHHHH!!!**'

Miss Gatling almost jumped on top of Mr
Grant and she clung to him, her long, bony
arms wrapped tightly round his rather portly
chest. Mr Grant couldn't have moved even if
he had wanted to. His arms were pinned
down each side of his body, and Miss Gatling
was staring over his shoulder at Jodie,
stupefied.

'Sorry,' said Jodie, a shade too cheerfully.

'Where's Mrs Farouk?' Miss Gatling
croaked, slowly letting go of Mr Grant and

searching round. A frightened squeak came from halfway up a nearby tree.

'Is it safe yet?' Mrs Farouk gingerly poked out her head from among the leaves, while Miss Gatling turned to Jodie and shook her head angrily.

'Don't you ever, EVER do that again!' she snapped.

This seemed most unfair to Jodie, who angrily banged her tail on the ground. 'You told me to do it!'

'I'm ringing your parents,' Miss Gatling said severely. 'I will not have a stegosaurus wandering about my school scaring everyone and eating the gardens. You should be in a zoo, not in a school.' The headteacher strode to her office, leaving Jodie gazing after her.

'This really is going to be a bad-hair day,' muttered Jodie, and she began chewing the grass on the school field.

3 A Visit to the Doctor

Mrs Bolton had to walk Jodie home at lunchtime. 'She's being excluded until she's normal,' were Miss Gatling's parting words.

'Normal?' muttered Mrs Bolton. 'Jodie's never been normal.'

'I heard that,' snorted Jodie as they walked down the road.

'Well, it's true,' sighed Mrs Bolton. 'Even when you were a baby you were awkward.'

'Babies are always awkward,' Jodie grumbled.

'I know they can be difficult, dear, but you did seem to be extra-difficult.'

'Oh? Like how?'

'When you'd only just been born and you were still in hospital, do you know, you wee-d all over the nurse when she was about to give you a bath. You slept all day and cried all night.'

Even to Jodie it seemed a bit extravagant and they didn't talk again until they met old Mr Parkinson, going off to the shops. Mr Parkinson stopped and gazed in awe through his thick glasses.

'My word, Mrs Bolton, that's some creature you've got there. What is it?'

Mrs Bolton gave an embarrassed cough. 'Um, it's a dog.'

'Woof,' said Jodie.

'There!' Mrs Bolton patted Jodie's back. 'Good dog.'

'What breed is it?' asked Mr Parkinson.

'Big,' Mrs Bolton replied quickly, and she hurried off with Jodie trotting beside her.

'You're ashamed of me, aren't you?' said Jodie. 'That's why you told him I was a dog. I bet you wish I really was a dog too.'

Mrs Bolton stopped short. She crouched down and held Jodie's head in her hands, looking straight into her eyes. 'Of course I don't, Jodie. How could you even think such a thing? I love you even when you're  grumpy. Just because we argue and get cross with you doesn't mean we don't love you. Anyhow, you joined in too. I thought it was very funny when you said "woof" – just like that – "woof"! We fooled Mr Parkinson.'

Jodie smiled. At least she sort of leered. She found that it was quite difficult to smile if you were a stegosaurus. Jodie thought that perhaps stegosauruses didn't have much to smile about. After all, as far as she could remember they had spent most of their time being chased and eaten by Tyrannosaurus rex. Maybe Mum was right. They *had* fooled Mr Parkinson, and it was funny.

When Mr Bolton got home in the evening, he told Jodie that he had made an appointment to see the doctor and after tea (more daisies) he took her down to the local surgery. It was strange in the waiting room though. The other people sat and stared at her, as if she'd made a nasty smell or something. Jodie ignored them and tried to concentrate on reading *Hello* magazine.

'What's wrong with her?' asked one lady, a bit sniffily.

'Mumps,' said Mr Bolton.

'Funny mumps,' muttered the lady.

'That's what they are,' Mr Bolton snapped back. 'Funny Mumps. There's an outbreak of them. Haven't you heard?'

The lady turned to the man sitting next to her. 'I've never seen mumps like that, have you?' The man shook his head and carried on reading his newspaper. 'That's not mumps,' insisted the lady. 'That's chickenpox.'

Jodie bristled with indignation. 'Chickenpox! Do you think I look like a chicken?'

'It's chickenpox,' the lady repeated.

Jodie raised her head, drew back her lips and growled, loudly. 'Raaargh!'

'It's mumps,' the lady hastily agreed, shooting out of her seat, 'and I suddenly feel a lot better. I think I may as well go home.' She hurried out without a backward glance.

Mr Bolton smiled and whispered into Jodie's scaly ear. 'That was a wicked thing to do.'

'She was being so stupid.'

Luckily they were saved from any further awkward encounters because they were called to the surgery. Jodie liked Doctor Singh, who had looked after her on several occasions when she had been ill.

'This is very unusual,' murmured Doctor Singh, as she listened to Jodie's heartbeat. 'I'm not sure if you should be here, or at the vet's! How do you feel, Jodie? Do you feel ill?'

'No, I feel fine. Actually in some ways it's quite nice being a dinosaur, but I'd prefer to be myself.'

Doctor Singh nodded. 'I'm sure you would, but I'm afraid I've never come across anything like this. I think you ought to go to the hospital and see a specialist – Mr

Pinkerton-Snark. He's an expert on rare diseases. Take this letter of introduction with you.'

So Mr Bolton and Jodie trailed up to the hospital, where Mr Pinkerton-Snark saw them at once, because it was such a peculiar case. In fact Mr Pinkerton-Snark was very excited by the whole business. He was a shiny man with a chubby, shining face and a shiny bald head. He even had two shiny gold teeth, and his gold-rimmed, half-moon glasses sparkled with pinpoints of light. He wore a dark suit, a striped shirt and a yellow bow tie. Jodie thought he looked more like an opera singer than a doctor.

Mr Pinkerton-Snark poked and prodded Jodie all over until she began to feel like a pincushion, while Mr Bolton watched and waited nervously. He kept asking what was wrong with his daughter, and at length Mr

Pinkerton-Snark announced his findings.

'She's a dinosaur,' he said.

'I would never have guessed,' Jodie
grumbled darkly.

'We know that, but *why* is she a dinosaur?'
said Mr Bolton.

'Huh!' squeaked the specialist. 'Why do
children do anything? They're a complete
mystery to me, but I have to say it is quite
fascinating. Most fascinating indeed. A real
dinosaur – a throwback to prehistoric times, a
link with our distant past. This is going to be

big news.' Mr Pinkerton-Snark was muttering quietly to himself and walking round Jodie, peering at her from all sides.

'Can you cure her?' asked Mr Bolton.

'She'll have to stay here.'

'What? Surely not? Can't I take her home?'

'Mister Bolton, your daughter has turned into a dinosaur. Suppose it's something catching? What if it's infectious? Do we want the streets full of dinosaurs? I don't think so. She will have to stay here so that I can run some tests and find out what is wrong with her and how to cure her.'

'I want to go home,' growled Jodie, who had taken an immediate dislike to Mr Pinkerton-Snark.

'You do want to be cured, don't you?' snapped the specialist.

Mr Bolton looked helplessly at Jodie.

'You'll be all right,' he said. 'You'll be well

looked after. We'll come and see you first thing in the morning. Is there anything you want us to bring? Pyjamas? Toothbrush?'

'Dinosaurs don't wear pyjamas, Dad, and I don't think they brush their teeth either. I would like my teddy though.'

Mr Bolton nodded. 'You will look after her?' he asked Mr Pinkerton-Snark, who was already hustling Jodie's father from the room.

'Jodie will be fine. You go home.'

Mr Bolton gave Jodie a hug and left, feeling a bit sad and guilty that he didn't have Jodie with him, but it was surely for the best? Little did Mr Bolton realize what Mr Pinkerton-Snark was already planning.

As soon as the specialist had set eyes on Jodie, he knew he was on to something big. A girl who had changed overnight into a stegosaurus? This was going to make medical history! He'd be famous – rich even! This was a story worth hundreds of thousands of pounds!

The first thing he had to do was make sure that he had Jodie safe and sound somewhere, away from the public, so that nobody else could get hold of the story. Then he could alert the newspapers and television and they would come swarming round like bees round a honey pot, with their cameras and microphones . . . and big fat wallets.

Mr Pinkerton-Snark led Jodie down endless corridors, until they reached a large room. On one side there was a little desk where a nurse sat on duty, wearing a crisply starched uniform. She looked more like a security guard than someone who was there to help the sick. In the middle of the room was a plastic tent, at least that's what Jodie thought it looked like.

Mr Pinkerton-Snark pushed back the heavy

plastic flaps. 'This is your new home,' he
announced.

'Lovely wallpaper,' said Jodie, staring at the
banks of machines lining each side.

'It's an Isolation Unit, that's all. It's where
we keep patients who might be very
infectious. Keep still while I fix these to your
body,' snapped Mr Pinkerton-Snark.

'What are they? What are you doing?'

'They're electrodes. They monitor your
heartbeat and your brainwaves and generally
keep an eye on how you are.' The electrodes
had coloured wires trailing from them into
the machines, and the machines blipped and
bleeped with a hundred and one dials and
little flickering screens. There was a constant
hum of electricity.

Jodie was overcome with lonely gloom and
she sank to the floor. Mr Pinkerton-Snark
smiled down at her and rubbed his hands

together. 'That's right, you settle down for a
good night's sleep. I have a lot of work to do.'

He chuckled quietly to himself. 'I've got big
plans for you and me. Do you think I like
looking after people with horrible spots and
nasty runny noses and spitty-sputtery coughs?
You must be joking! But you! You're something

quite special, and you are going to be my goose that lays the golden egg.'

Jodie was puzzled. Why did chubby-chops think she was a goose all of a sudden? But she was too weary and miserable to comment.

Mr Pinkerton-Snark pushed his way out of the tent. He was going to be famous! He would go down in history as the first doctor to treat this astonishing new disease. 'I shall call it Dinosaur Pox,' he smiled to himself.

Jodie listened to the specialist's footsteps as they receded down the corridor. She lay slumped in the corner, in a nest of trailing wires. She had hated her hair and she had hated her freckles, but surely that was better than being a stegosaurus? A small tear began to well up in her left eye.

Dinosaurs couldn't smile, but they could cry.

4 Mark to the Rescue

The Boltons went back to the hospital that evening to deliver Jodie's teddy. Mark came with them. He was shocked when he saw the condition his sister was in, surrounded by bleeping machines, and with wires stuck all over her.

'Wow!' he breathed. 'You look like Frankenstein.'

'Thank you, Mark. It's so sweet of you to say so,' Jodie answered, a trifle coldly.

'No, I mean – weird!' Mark shook his head in disbelief. 'It's horrible.'

'All for her own good,' said Mr Pinkerton-Snark with a cheerful smile.

'When will they let you come home?' asked Mark.

'That's a stupid question,' snorted the specialist.

'He is only nine.' Mrs Bolton was apologetic.

'And he's not stupid either,' growled Jodie, which pleased Mark mightily, since she had never, ever admitted such a possibility before.

Mr Pinkerton-Snark folded his arms and looked down at Jodie's brother. 'Look at the condition she's in. She's a menace to the general public. There is no question of her going home.'

'You can't keep her here for ever!'

'And since when have you been a doctor, young man?' This stinging rebuke silenced Mark for the time being, and the specialist drew Mr and Mrs Bolton to one side to have a private word with them.

Mark stepped closer to the plastic tent. 'Are you all right?' His voice had dropped to a secretive whisper.

'I'm bored. There isn't even a telly here.'

'Is there anything I can do?'

'You?' Jodie gave a choking laugh. 'Like what?'

'If you're going to be like that . . .' Mark said moodily. 'I was only trying to help you.'

'Thanks for nothing.'

Mark gave up. Obviously Jodie was going into one of her most grumpy moods, and if that was the case it wouldn't be worth speaking to her for hours. All the same, he was appalled at the way she was being kept, all wired up, like some hideous experiment.

'I wish she could come home,' said Mark, on the way back to the house.

Mrs Bolton gave him a ghost of a smile. 'You and Jodie are always quarrelling. How come you want her back home?'

Mark shrugged. 'I suppose I miss her. I mean, we *liked* to quarrel. That's what brothers and sisters do, isn't it? I bet you quarrelled with Uncle Nick when you were small.'

Mark was right. Mrs Bolton had spent half her childhood arguing and fighting with her older brother. Mark went on. 'Anyway, I miss her, and I don't like to see her in hospital like that. We ought to go back and rescue her.'

'I know how you feel,' said Mr Bolton, 'but we can't barge into the hospital and rescue her. It's hard to understand, but hospital is the best place for her at present. Mr Pinkerton-Snark is trying to cure her.'

Mark scowled. Why did parents have to be sensible all the time? This wasn't the time to be sensible. They had to *do* something.

When he went to bed he lay there tossing

and turning for ages, his brain humming with a thousand thoughts. He couldn't leave Jodie like that. He kept thinking of her in her tent, all alone. Mark knew how he would feel if he were in her place, and he couldn't bear to think of Jodie feeling *that* bad.

At two o'clock in the morning he got out of bed. He gazed out of his window into the dark and silent street. It was no good. He had to rescue his sister.

Mark dressed quickly and tiptoed downstairs. He carefully let himself out through the back door, grabbed his bicycle from the shed and set off for the hospital. He didn't even put on his lights because he didn't want to be seen, and his heart beat wildly. Supposing he was spotted by a passing police car, or someone saw him, riding like a Fury with no lights?

At last he reached the hospital, hid his bicycle deep among some bushes and crept across to the Isolation Unit. The corridor was empty, and Mark slipped down it quickly. When he reached the unit he peered carefully round the open door. Mark could hardly believe his luck. The nurse was fast asleep with her head and arms spread across her desk. She was snoring.

Hardly daring to breathe, Mark crept across the room and carefully slipped through the plastic flaps. Jodie opened one eye and then very quickly followed with the other.

'Ssssh!' hissed Mark, as he began removing the electrodes. The dials and lights went into a terminal nosedive. 'You've just died!' grinned Mark. 'Come on, it's time to go home.'

Jodie struggled to her feet and followed Mark as he led the way out of the tent and past the sleeping nurse. They crept fearfully down the corridor, and Mark kept glancing back, but there was still no sign of the nurse waking. They reached the double doors at the end of the corridor, pushed them open and they were free.

'This way,' said Mark, and hurried to retrieve his bicycle.

Jodie set off at a gallop, moving her heavy body through the dark night with surprising speed. Every time they saw the lights of

approaching cars they quickly hid – behind hedges or walls, or just crouching in the black shadows.

Mark's heart was racing with excitement, and Jodie too felt a thrill as they made their getaway. It was only when they had almost reached home that Jodie suddenly had a thought that threw her into panic and she stumbled to a halt.

'Stop!' she panted. 'Listen, I don't think this is a good idea.'

'You're not going back to the hospital! Jodie, you can be *so* stupid!'

'Of course I'm not going back, but I don't think we should go home. What happens when the nurse wakes up and realizes I've gone? Alarms will go off. Pinkerton-Snark will come looking. They'll all come looking, and where's the first place they'll look?'

Mark gulped. Jodie was absolutely right. The first place they would look would be back at the house. Then they would take Jodie away again and that would be that. On the other hand, what were they supposed to do?

'We've got to find somewhere to hide out,' said Jodie. 'Somewhere people won't think of looking.'

'The old railway yard?' suggested Mark.

'You know, the one we drive past when we go to the shopping centre. It's not used any more. It's just derelict buildings and there are loads of them. There must be one that we can hide in. We'll stop at the house first, just for a second, so I can pick up some food.'

Jodie nodded and, keeping to the shadows, they made their way first to the house, and then on to the railway yard. By the time they reached it, dawn was beginning to tinge the darkness with a streak of blue and pink. They found an old brick shed and at last they were able to sit down and relax.

They were both tired, especially Mark. Being up so late, and having such excitement had really worn him out. He rested back against one wall and Jodie trotted over to him. 'I hated it there. I never did like Winky-Pinky. Thanks for getting me out.'

'I was going to take you home,' said Mark.

'I don't know what we're going to do now. This wasn't in my plan.'

'Don't worry. We'll think of something. You get some sleep. I'll keep watch for a couple of hours, and then you can take over while I sleep.'

'You sure?'

'Yeah, go on, you go to sleep.'

Mark rolled gratefully on to his side, closed his eyes, and was soon snoring. Jodie hated to admit it, but she was glad he was with her. She needed the company, and nobody else understood how she felt about things. She wasn't too sure that Mark did for that matter, but she did know that he saw the problems the same way she did. They had to keep one step ahead; they had to remain free.

She stared out at the big yard. In the growing light she could make out a lovely bunch of fresh green nettles. They looked absolutely scrumptious. If only it was all over. When it was all over they'd go back home.

Home. Jodie had no idea how long it would take, or what would happen, but she longed to be able to walk through the front door and say 'Hello everyone – it's me – I'm home!' as if nothing had happened. She had a bizarre thought. *I haven't got my door key.* Sadly, Jodie leaned her heavy head against the edge of the door and gazed out at the deserted yard.

5 The Hunt Begins

Mr Pinkerton-Snark was not a happy man. He strode down the hospital corridor with a tearful nurse trailing in his wake. 'I don't know how it happened,' cried the nurse. 'She was asleep.'

'*You* were asleep!' roared the irate specialist. 'And now we have a dinosaur on the loose. Do you realize my career has probably just run out of this hospital, right under your nose?'

'I don't know what you mean,' stuttered the unfortunate nurse.

'Of course you don't,' sneered Pinkerton-Snark, 'and do you know why you don't know? It's because you're STUPID!'

The specialist banged through some doors and strode into his office. 'I shall have to call in the police. Soon the whole town will know. We shan't be able to keep this a secret any longer.' Moments later he was on the phone to the police, explaining everything, and still desperately hoping that he might be able to get the stegosaurus back before the newspapers got on to the story.

'She'll have headed straight for home,' he said. 'But there might be trouble. If she's escaped it means that she won't want to come back here quietly. Her parents could prove awkward too. They're rather over-protective. You know how parents are sometimes – too stupid to understand what's going on . . . Yes, I'll meet you over there, and make sure you have plenty of officers.'

Mr Pinkerton-Snark slammed down the telephone and glared at the night nurse.

'You're fired,' he snapped. 'If – IF – I get my dinosaur back, I might just reconsider your position, but in the meantime I don't want to see your useless face here again. Pack your thermometer and go.'

The poor nurse burst into tears all over again and flung herself at the specialist's feet. 'Please, please,' she cried. 'I've got two children at home I'm trying to bring up, and their dad left home months ago . . . Please!'

She clung to the specialist's left leg and as he tried to leave his office she was dragged along the floor by his leg, like a wailing mop. Her pleas fell on deaf ears and Pinkerton-Snark finally managed to shake her off and leave her lying in a sobbing heap, while he hurried to his car and went racing off to the Boltons' house to recapture his prize.

The police had already arrived and were piling out of a big black van, which had POLICE UNDERCOVER TEAM written down each side. Now they were hammering on the door loudly enough to wake the dead, let alone the sleeping. Mr Bolton came hurrying down in his dressing gown and opened the door, only to have a flashlight shone directly into his face. He staggered back as policemen poured into the house and began a frantic search.

'What's going on?' cried Mr Bolton, while Mrs Bolton stared anxiously over his shoulder. Pinkerton-Snark turned on him.

'Your daughter has escaped,' he hissed.

'Jodie?' Mrs Bolton pulled the collar of her gown round her neck. 'Is she all right?'

'You tell me,' snapped Pinkerton-Snark.

'What do you mean by that?'

'Where is she? Where are you hiding her?'

A great crashing noise came from upstairs as the house was ransacked in the desperate search.

'I don't know what you're talking about,' said Mr Bolton.

'WHERE IS SHE?' roared the specialist, pushing his face close up against Mr Bolton's.

'I DON'T KNOW!' Mr Bolton roared back. 'And don't you try to bully me!'

Mr Pinkerton-Snark's eyes narrowed. 'You're all in this together, aren't you?'

At that moment, several policemen came crashing back down the stairs. 'No dinosaur here,' reported one. 'There's nobody else upstairs.'

Mrs Bolton shot a worried glance at her husband. Nobody? What about Mark? She

went up the stairs two at a
time and threw herself into
his room. It was empty.
Mrs Bolton came back out,
white as a sheet, and stood
at the top of the stairs.

'Mark's gone too,' she
whispered.

Mr Pinkerton-Snark
smiled. Now they were
getting somewhere. He turned to the
Inspector in charge of the police, who still
had his pyjamas on underneath his raincoat.
'They're all in this together. They've freed the
dinosaur from hospital and now the boy is
hiding her somewhere.'

'Don't be ridiculous!' Mr Bolton was
furious. 'Do you think we'd let a nine-year-old
boy go out at dead of night, with or without a
dinosaur?'

60

Inspector Craw, a tired, grey man with a thin face and thinner hair, stifled a yawn and nodded. 'The gentleman does have a point. My guess is that this was the boy's idea, and these people didn't know anything about it.'

'Hmmm. Maybe – and if that is the case then it shouldn't be too difficult to find them,' claimed the specialist. 'A small boy and a dinosaur will soon give themselves away. We'll have them back in no time. Come on, Inspector, there's no time to lose.' And the poor inspector, still blinking sleep from his eyes, was hauled away by the eager specialist.

Mr and Mrs Bolton stood at the door and watched the police cars swirl away in a flurry of flashing lights. Mr Bolton put an arm round his wife's shoulders. 'There's something fishy about that specialist. He's more like a shark than a snark. You know what I wanted to do? Pull his big nose right off his face! Well done, Mark,' he muttered proudly. 'I do hope they're OK.'

When Mark woke, bright sunlight was flooding the derelict yard. He stirred, opened his eyes and gazed across at his sister.

'I'm hungry,' she growled. 'What about you?'

'Starving. Let's have some food.' He rummaged inside his rucksack, pulling out several tins and placing them in a neat row along the floor.

Jodie looked at them, mournfully reading the labels to herself. 'Baked beans with sausage, chunky chicken casserole, frankfurters, meatballs! I'm a vegetarian, Mark. Stegosauruses are herbivores. We eat vegetables.'

'Oh, yes, sorry, I forgot.' He gazed gloomily inside his rucksack. 'It doesn't

matter anyway. I haven't got a tin-opener.'

Jodie almost exploded. 'Haven't got a tin-opener? You're supposed to be helping me and you're about as much use as a wet paper bag.' She began lifting her feet and stamping on the ground with frustration.

Mark glanced round the derelict shed. 'No wood,' he muttered, 'and I forgot the matches. I haven't got anything to cook with either.' He looked helplessly at his sister.

'This is too much! No tin-opener! No stove! What is the point in being rescued by the most useless rescuer in the entire history of rescuing?'

'I've got a torch,' Mark added lamely.

Jodie finally lost her cool. She thundered angrily about the shed, banging up against the walls with all her impressive weight and making them shudder. She barged into Mark several times, shoving him around with her head and grunting crossly. Finally, Jodie went and threw her bulk into a dingy corner, where she lay regarding her brother with angry, accusing eyes. Mark was hopeless. She was helpless. Everything was pointless.

Mark waited until she had calmed down a bit. 'I shall have to go and get some food.' Jodie lifted her head in alarm. Mark could see the panic in her eyes. 'I'll be careful. We're pretty close to the Retail Park here. I'll slip into the supermarket, nobody will notice. At least I remembered my pocket money.' He fished inside one trouser pocket, pulling out a ten pound note and several coins and counting it, while Jodie watched with growing interest.

'How come you've got so much dosh? That's absolutely typical. You've always got more money than me. How do you do it?'

'Does it matter?' said Mark. 'You're a dinosaur now. Dinosaurs don't go shopping.'

What have I done to deserve this? That's what Jodie kept asking herself now. She thought she had been fed up before, when all she had to fret over were freckles and curly hair. She thought her life had been miserable before, when all she had was a brother to quarrel with and parents who wouldn't be what she wanted them to be. She had thought that it would surely be wonderful to be big and strong and powerful.

But it wasn't wonderful, not really . . . not

at all, in fact, if she was honest with herself. (And this was probably a first for Jodie.) She didn't like being the only stegosaurus in the world, being *that* kind of special, being the centre of so much attention. Jodie was beginning to look back on her pre-stegosaurus days as a golden carefree time.

It was too late now. She was a prehistoric dinosaur, two-metres long and one-and-a-half-metres high, with purple blotches instead of freckles and great fat scaly plates instead of her curly black hair. She stepped closer to Mark, pressing up against his legs and gazing up at him with mournful eyes. She let out a long, long sigh, a heavy rush of air from the depths of her dinosaur belly, and laid her head across his feet.

Mark bent down and stroked the tough skin on her head. 'I guess it's not much fun,' he said. 'Look, I'll be as quick as I can, and

very, very careful.' He checked through the
crack, pulled the door a bit wider and slipped
out into the warm sunshine.

The fresh air hit his face and perked him
up in an instant. Stepping away from the old
building he realized that Jodie smelled. Fond
as he was of his sister (with the kind of
fondness great quarrellers always have for
each other), he had to admit she was getting
stinky. He took a deep breath and hurried off
to the supermarket.

6 Twinkletoes Makes a Mistake

Never had a supermarket seemed so dangerous. Mark's eyes darted about as he watched for any signs of approaching trouble. Every person he saw seemed a potential threat, but as time passed and they completely ignored him he began to relax a little. He was glad to find the supermarket thronging with people. He felt safer among so many – less likely to be noticed.

He picked out some ready-made sandwiches for himself and then spent a long time wandering about in the vegetable section, pondering over what he should get Jodie. At one point a young assistant approached him, sending Mark's heart into overdrive as he panicked about being caught, but she only wanted to know if she could help.

'You seem a bit lost,' she said cheerfully. 'I thought maybe you were looking for something in particular?'

This was quite true, but how could Mark say yes, he wanted something for a stegosaurus waiting in a derelict shed by the railway line?

'Thanks, but I'm just browsing,' he muttered, and then he had a bright idea. 'Actually I've got to feed my guinea pig.'

'I used to have a guinea pig!' said the assistant. 'He was called Sniffer. He was black and white. What's yours called?'

'Oh, er, Twinkletoes,' Mark said quickly, as a vision of Jodie's elephantine feet flashed through his mind. 'She's purple, I mean brown.' He hurriedly grabbed two bumper packs of carrots, a big savoy cabbage and a

giant bag of potatoes that he could barely lift. 'These will be fine,' he said.

The girl laughed. 'Is that *all* for your guinea pig? She must be very big.'

'She's the biggest I've ever seen,' Mark answered evenly. 'And when she's eaten this lot, she'll be even bigger.' He marched off to the till and paid, leaving the surprised assistant wondering if she should have fed her guinea pig on potatoes.

Back at the shed, Jodie waited, staring wistfully at the big nettle patch. It was so near. It was so juicy. She could even smell it from her hiding place. The old railway yard was completely quiet and quite deserted. There wasn't a single house near by.

Her stomach rumbled loudly. She nuzzled at the opening, pushing the door further open. What lovely, luscious scents filtered across her sensitive nostrils! *If I make a quick run at them*, she thought, *I can grab a mouthful and get back here in a jiffy and no harm done.*

Jodie fixed her eyes on the nettle patch and began a mini countdown. Three, two, one, go! She dashed out, thundering the short distance across the concrete to the nettles, where she grabbed a huge mouthful, skidded on two fat legs and went rushing back to the shed. Brilliant! She chewed ecstatically on the tough nettle leaves and in too short a time they had vanished down her throat, leaving her even more hungry.

Well, if it worked once, it could work twice. Three, two, one, go! Again Jodie plunged out from the shed, hurtled across to the nettles, seized a bunch and charged merrily back to the shed. A minute passed and then out she came for a third time, pounding across the yard and back to the shed.

In the far corner of the railway yard an elderly man was walking his dog. He stopped and watched with mounting disbelief as a

dinosaur hurtled out from an old railway shed, grabbed some nettles and disappeared back in again. He watched the dinosaur do this three times, and then hurried home.

A full-scale search was well under way. Police were scouting the streets and conducting house-to-house inquiries. The Boltons' telephone hardly stopped ringing as inquisitive neighbours rang in to say how sorry they were, could they do anything to help, and was it because of the dog?

'What dog?' asked Mr Bolton.

'Why, the one Mr Parkinson saw yesterday.'

Mrs Bolton smiled and mouthed across at her husband. 'Big dog,' she said. 'It's a new breed.'

'No, it wasn't a dog,' scowled Mr Bolton. 'Now please get off the telephone. If you want to help you can stop ringing us.'

'I was only trying to help,' the caller said, indignantly.

'No, you weren't, you were being nosy,' answered Mr Bolton, and he slammed down the telephone. Mrs Bolton put a calming hand on his arm. 'Honestly,' he fumed.

Meanwhile, Inspector Craw and Mr Pinkerton-Snark were still crawling round the town in a squad car, hoping to spot the elusive dinosaur. The specialist was becoming increasingly impatient. If only they had a clue, a lead, a sighting. The inspector was sitting in the back, his head nodding forward dozily on to his chest. A message came crackling through on the radio.

'Calling Craw, calling Craw. Dinosaur spotted down at the old railway yard.'

Inspector Craw jerked awake and hastily scribbled some notes as more details came through over the radio.

'At last!' cried Pinkerton-Snark.

'Old man out walking his dog saw it, three times,' repeated the inspector. 'He's certain it was a dinosaur. Says it was running about eating nettles. There's a car on the way there now, but we're even closer, so let's go!'

The car's siren began howling like a tortured ghost. They raced down the road and skidded round corners, leaving a trail of black tyre marks and a strong smell of burnt rubber.

Inside the old railway shed, Jodie heard the wail of approaching sirens and was immediately afraid. She nuzzled with her snout at the door, peering out. She knew that police cars were hurtling closer and closer, and that could only mean one thing – they were after her.

Her blood ran hot and cold. Someone must have seen her when she went out for the nettles. Where, oh where, was Mark? He'd been gone for ages.

And then Jodie saw him, staggering across the concrete towards the shed, dragging his bag of vegetables with him. He didn't seem to have heard the police cars that were screaming nearer and nearer.

Jodie felt powerless. She must stay hidden, but at any moment Mark would either be caught or he would give away her hiding place. Inside her massive ribcage her dinosaur heart was thundering furiously. The passing seconds became hours, like watching a film in slow motion.

All at once, a squad car hurtled into the yard, slewing across the rubbly concrete.

'That's the boy!' cried Pinkerton-Snark. 'Over there with the bags. Pick him up, sergeant.'

Mark turned and watched as the police car

rushed towards him. He looked all around, but there was nobody else they could possibly be after. His heart sank to his boots. The Undercover Squad squealed into the yard in their black van and raced towards him, closely followed by another squad car. Meanwhile the first car had slid to a halt and out jumped Inspector Craw and Mr Pinkerton-Snark.

'Don't move, Mark! Stay there! You're coming with us.'

Mark froze. He stared wildly across to the shed, just able to make out Jodie's eyes glinting anxiously behind the closed doors. At least nobody knew where his sister was yet. He prepared to make a run for it. He reckoned that if he couldn't avoid capture he might at least be able to lure the hunters away from Jodie and give her time to escape. Above his head a police helicopter rocked

slowly as it descended, pressing a gale of wind
down on Mark.

'Just keep very still!' boomed Mr Pinkerton-
Snark, 'and you'll be all right.'

Inspector Craw spoke to his team. 'We've
got the boy, and the dinosaur is bound to be
near by. Spread out and search the sheds.'

Policemen began running to the buildings
and Mark anxiously bit his lip. What could he
do?

'There's a good boy,' called Mr Pinkerton-Snark. 'Come on, over here.'

A good boy! How pathetic! The police were edging closer to Jodie's hiding place, and Pinkerton-Snark was closing in on Mark. He had to do something, before it was too late. If only he could draw the police away from the shed. He suddenly dropped his bags, turned and sprinted for the far side of the yard.

'After him!' yelled the specialist, and the police turned and stared at Mark's rapidly disappearing figure.

'Get the boy! He must know where the dinosaur is hiding!' cried Inspector Craw, and the police raced back to their cars.

Tyres squealed as three vehicles roared across the yard, with policemen leaning out of windows, yelling at Mark. Doors flew open and several policemen leaped out and hurled themselves after Mark, who was running like the wind. His heart felt about to burst.

'Can't catch me!' he yelled over his shoulder, and then 'Ooof!' He hurtled straight into the waiting arms of the police gorilla, two-metres tall and built like the Empire State Building.

Jodie watched in despair. It could only end one way. The big figures of the adults seemed to converge from all sides on her hapless brother and they pounced, while he kicked and screamed. 'Let me go! I'm innocent! I want to see my solicitor!'

This was too much. With a terrifying roar, Jodie exploded from the shed.

7 Jodie to the Rescue

'Raaaaargh!' One door
went flying across the
yard in splinters while
the other flapped
brokenly for a few
seconds before toppling
to the ground with a
loud crash. Jodie was

already galloping furiously across the yard in
a cloud of whirling dust. Her thick, fat legs
made the concrete surface shudder and crack.
She opened her powerful jaws wide and
bellowed again. 'Raaaaaargh!'

By the time Mark's captors spotted her, it
was too late. She thundered into their midst,
sending them flying with a toss of her head, a
painful flick of her thick tail, or a side-swipe

with her belly. The air was thick with painful cries as they crashed sprawling to the ground, or flew gracelessly through the air.

Mark grabbed hold of one of Jodie's fins, hauled himself on to her back and away they galloped, leaving a moaning, groaning heap of helpless hunters struggling on the ground.

Only Mr Pinkerton-Snark seemed unscathed by Jodie's devastating attack. He gazed after the disappearing dinosaur with a look of triumph. 'She won't escape me this time. Come on, Craw!' He grabbed the dazed inspector, who was trying to stifle a nosebleed, and tried to drag him by the collar to a waiting car.

Jodie pounded across the big yard, hot snorts of breath bursting from her nostrils. Mark clung on for dear life, bouncing about like a rag doll. Jodie headed for the yard exit, but even as she caught a distant glimpse of the brightly shining superstores, a fourth police car roared down the road.

Jodie took no notice and simply carried on, well into her stride. The car screeched and swerved sharply to avoid crashing head first into the stegosaurus. Rapidly it slewed round and came after her in hot pursuit, lights flashing and siren sawing the air into heavy chunks.

As Jodie thundered on to the road, it drew up alongside, with two policemen leaning out of their windows and yelling at Mark. 'Stop! You haven't got a hope of escaping!'

Mark was too busy clinging to his sister's back to pay any attention to what was happening next to him, but Jodie was well aware of the danger. The car kept swerving towards her in a very threatening manner, trying to push her off the road and force her up against a wall.

By this time, Jodie was well aware how strong and heavy she was. She was built like a small tank, and as the car lunged towards her again she threw her own full, thundering weight against the vehicle. Her attack was a complete surprise, and the car bounced away out of control and decided to attack the brick wall head-on. It lost.

Three policemen staggered from their suddenly foreshortened vehicle. They clung to each other in a daze, and then collapsed in a heap against the wall, while the siren coughed, peeped and finally gave up the ghost altogether.

In the meantime, Inspector Craw appeared to be doing an impression of a hyperactive windmill as he fought his way out of the clutches of Mr Pinkerton-Snark. He practically fell out of the police car.

'Gerroff!' shouted the inspector. 'I'm going in the helicopter!'

He waved down the chopper and climbed on board. He quickly regained his calm, carefully following the battle below. He gave curt orders over the radio and dabbed at his bruised nose with a blood-stained hanky.

Jodie was clear of the cars for the time being. She had almost reached the superstores. Her hope now was that she could somehow lose her pursuers in the crowded shopping area. Unfortunately she was not expecting a clattering helicopter to swoop down on her like some fearfully large and noisy vulture. Jodie swerved away and went pounding straight into the supermarket.

Chaos! Shoppers scattered in every direction, and if they didn't scatter fast enough they simply went flying as Jodie blundered down one aisle, up another, down another.

Mark clung to her back with aching hands and shouted apologies over his fleeing shoulder as shoppers fell like ninepins. 'Oops! Sorry! So sorry! Uh-oh – there goes another one – sorry! Beg your pardon!'

His apologies were drowned by a rising cacophony of screams, yells, cries and sobs, not to mention Jodie's raspy breathing and her frequent grunts and roars. High up inside his office the panic-stricken General Manager was calling the Emergency Services.

'Yes!' he yelled down the telephone. 'You

heard me right the first time – I did say there's a dinosaur on the rampage! For heaven's sake get here quickly before someone gets killed!'

This last remark was a bit hard on Jodie and it was a good thing she didn't hear it. Despite the mess she was making, she was taking as much care as a speeding dinosaur could to avoid mowing down too many people. This generally meant mowing down stacks of tins, and mounds of fruit and vegetables instead.

She even managed to produce a wonderful domino effect when she unfortunately sent an entire row of shelving toppling to one side, spilling its goods across the floor before it hit the next row and sent that plunging too. The second row collapsed against a third row and so on, until in the end seven rows of shelving had been totally demolished – not that anyone was actually counting. They were too busy screaming and running away as fast as possible.

By the time Jodie managed to find the exit, she had reduced the inside of the giant store to a heaving ocean of struggling people, squashed vegetables, dented tins, split containers, broken biscuits, and a general mishmash of spoiled goods. Leaving the mini-earthquake behind, Jodie went thundering out of the exit.

Waiting outside were five squad cars and a hovering helicopter.

'Give yourself up!' boomed Inspector Craw through the loud hailer. 'There's no way out!'

From all sides Mark could hear the sound of approaching sirens. His heart sank. The entire police force must be after them, he reckoned, but he was wrong. It wasn't just the police force. The fire brigade was on its way too, and they were being closely followed by a convoy of ambulances, just in case.

They all arrived at the same time, piling into the Retail Park with lights flashing and sirens blaring. Jodie took all this in at one glance and plunged into the nearby Garden Centre.

Miss Gatling was looking for geraniums. She liked geraniums. In fact Miss Gatling liked everything about gardening. It was a pleasant, relaxing hobby. Flowers, unlike children, usually did what they were told. Miss Gatling enjoyed browsing in the local

Garden Centre, where everything was so quiet and peaceful. Unfortunately, Miss Gatling was about to be rudely awakened from her state of bliss. Jodie and Mark were thundering towards her at top speed. Miss Gatling heard the noise and turned. She froze. Her eyes popped. Her jaw dropped, and then dropped a bit more, and then even more still. There was a dinosaur charging straight at her. Miss Gatling's face set in a stern mask and she pointed a stiff, thin finger at the dino-tank.

'Jodie Bolton! Stop that at once!' But Jodie couldn't stop. She had twenty-five policemen, Pinkerton-Snark, eighteen firemen and six stretcher-bearers chasing right behind her.

'Get out of the way!' yelled Mark. 'Or you'll get run over!'

'How dare you speak to me like that, young man. If you don't stop at once I shall . . .

Ohhhhhhhhh!
Aaaaaaaaah!
Ooooooooo!
Eeeeeeeee!' The
headteacher went
flying into the air,
executed a
rumbustious
somersault, which
showed her thermal

underwear in a most unladylike manner –
and then plunged headfirst into the display
pond. By the time she surfaced, Jodie was
already far away, bumbling against big potted
plants and generally creating havoc.

She was tired. Her fat legs ached and she
felt as if she couldn't run another step. Jodie
desperately searched for a hiding place. She
crashed through one last display of plants,
sending them spilling on all sides and found

herself at the back of the Garden Centre. In front of her was a solid brick wall. Wearily she turned, only to find a packed crowd of excited shoppers hemming her in on all sides.

Jodie snorted threateningly and pawed the ground. The crowd stopped. They did not dare come any closer, and Jodie didn't go anywhere near them.

Mark leaned forward, putting his head close to Jodie's. 'I think we've hit a problem.'

'What? Only one?' panted Jodie.

There was a disturbance at the back of the crowd and moments later Inspector Craw pushed to the front, along with several policemen. 'It's all over,' he said. 'Get off the beast, Mark.'

'She's not a beast! She's my sister!' This remark was greeted with howls of laughter by the crowd. Mark didn't care. What did they know about it?

Inspector Craw shrugged his shoulders and ordered his men forward. As they approached they unravelled a rope net, grasping the weighted end. They fanned out and spread right round Jodie on all sides. She lifted her head and roared. 'Raaaargh!'

Mr Pinkerton-Snark could hardly contain himself. 'Wonderful, wonderful – she roars as well! I do hope she does it on television!'

The heavy net flew through the air. It spread out like a dark thundercloud, pinning Mark to his sister's back, and bringing Jodie to her knees. She thought of struggling, but there was little point. She was almost relieved that she didn't have to run any more.

'It's all over, Mark,' she murmured.

'Get the boy out of here,' snarled Pinkerton-Snark, and a police officer began freeing Mark from the coils of the net. Pinkerton-Snark turned to the inspector. 'We need a truck. We'll use one of the fork-lift vehicles from the Garden Centre to load the creature on to the truck.'

'Where do we take her?'

'She'll have to go to the Animal Quarantine Hospital.'

'The one they use in case an animal has rabies?'

'Exactly. They should have a cage that's large enough.'

'You can't do that!' yelled Mark. 'She's my sister! We want to go home!' He leaped at Pinkerton-Snark and began pummelling the specialist with his fist. A police sergeant hurried forward and grabbed him. He snaked one arm round Mark's waist and pulled him away. Mark kicked furiously.

Inspector Craw fixed Mark with a stern eye. 'Your parents are worried stiff about the pair of you. Take him to the squad car,

sergeant, I'll be along as soon as I've cleared the area and seen this dinosaur safely off to quarantine.'

'No!' yelled Mark, as he was dragged away, 'I want to be with my sister!'

The crowd parted as the sergeant and another officer pulled and pushed and dragged Mark off. He caught one last glimpse of Jodie lying there under the net all alone, then the crowd joined together like a wall, and she was gone.

8 Strange Business in the Night

It was evening before the Boltons were allowed to visit Jodie. She was being kept in a cage. Mr Pinkerton-Snark had organized a press conference for the following morning, and he was looking forward to it. Tomorrow his name would be known worldwide. Tomorrow he would be rich. He had gone off to the hospital to hand in his resignation. He wouldn't need to work ever again.

Mrs Bolton wiped a tear from her cheek and clutched the cage bars. 'Oh Jodie, we do love you, you know. We've always loved you. There was no need for this – we loved you just as you were.'

Jodie's head lifted a fraction. 'I know,' she said, fighting back some tears of her own.

Her father cleared his throat noisily. 'We'll get you out somehow,' he said. 'We'll get you back to normal.' He forced a smile. 'I want my funny freckle-face back.'

'I never had *funny* freckles,' said Jodie. 'But they were better than this.'

Mr Bolton held up a sack. 'We brought you some carrots,' he said, and he tipped most of them into the cage before pushing the rest of the sack through after them.

'Oh yummy,' growled Jodie, turning her back on the pile. Mr Bolton fished for his wife's hand and squeezed it. Neither of them knew what to say.

Mark leaned against the bars. 'I'm sorry about this morning,' he said. 'We never made it.'

'It was brilliant,' said Jodie. 'I quite enjoyed myself. What a mess we made! Anyhow, thanks for helping me escape and everything.'

'It's OK.' Mark shrugged. 'You would have done the same for me.'

Would she? Jodie wasn't sure. Well, maybe.

'You'll be on telly tomorrow,' he went on.

'I don't want to be on telly. Do you think I want the whole world to see me like this?'

'Well, *you* changed into a dinosaur, so why don't you just change back?'

'Got a magic wand, have you?' snorted Jodie.

'Who's a grumpy guinea pig?' Mark muttered and turned his back on her.

Sometimes there was no pleasing his sister. On the other hand he didn't want it to end like this. He turned round again. 'I wish you were back home, I mean not as you are now, you know, as you were.'

'Mark, you didn't like me as I was. We were always quarrelling.'

'Yeah, I know, but . . .' He struggled for words. 'It was OK, wasn't it? I mean we quarrelled, but everyone does that. I never wanted you to be a dinosaur.'

'Snap!' grunted Jodie

'. . . and I wish you weren't. I just want you back home.'

'We all want you back, just as you were,' added Mrs Bolton.

Jodie lifted her heavy head and looked at her family, gathered together on the other side of the bars.

Mr Bolton forced a smile. 'We'll come and

see you first thing in the morning. Shall I bring some more carrots? Courgettes maybe, or turnips?'

'I'm OK,' mumbled Jodie. She slumped down on to one side and stretched out her wrinkled neck. 'I'm tired. I'm going to sleep. See you tomorrow.'

The Boltons walked away and left her there, half asleep, but still thinking to herself: *I want to get out of this. I don't like being a stegosaurus any more. I want to be Jodie. I don't mind freckles. I promise I won't complain about black, curly hair ever again. I just want to be me. I'll even be nice to Mark – well, sometimes, possibly, now and then, if I remember in time.*

When the Boltons reached home they went about things very quietly, each one lost in their own thoughts about Jodie.

Mark sat on the edge of his bed with his

hands in his lap, feeling nervous and embarrassed. He wasn't at all sure whether he believed in God or not. He had never made a private prayer before and now he looked vaguely upwards as if God might be hovering invisibly round his ceiling somewhere.

'Dear God, if you're there, please listen, and if you're not then you won't hear anyway so I don't suppose it matters, but will you please help Jodie? She's in dead trouble right now. She doesn't want to be a dinosaur any longer. If you can change her back to herself I promise I'll be nice to her and I won't call her "Spotty", or quarrel with her ever again – at least I shall try not to, but you mustn't mind if I forget sometimes because she really can be dreadful to live with. I'm sure you couldn't put up with her for long, but please help her even if she is horrible to me.'

He paused a few moments and then added:
'Oh yes, if you *can* change her back, could
you give her long, straight hair this time?
She'd like that. She'd prefer to be blonde, but
I don't suppose she'll be too fussy. Thanks.'

Mark climbed under his duvet and drifted
into a fitful sleep, dreaming about evil doctors
and dinosaurs. He had gone to sleep
worrying about Jodie, and he was still
worrying about her in his dreams. He wished

that he could think of some way to rescue her, change her back, and get her away from the odious Pinkerton-Snark.

He was woken at three in the morning by pebbles rattling against his window. He struggled out of his covers with a pounding heart, rushed to the window, flung it wide, and received a face full of grit for his trouble. He blinked angrily as a tall dark shape emerged from the shadows.

'Mark?'

'Jodie! Is that you? I mean the real you?'

'Of course it's me. Who else were you expecting – Father Christmas? Four times I've thrown pebbles at your window. I thought you'd never wake up.'

'But what happened? How did you –?'

'I'll tell you later. There's no time now. Hurry up and let me in, I need some proper clothes. I'm wearing a carrot sack, and it's smelly and not terribly fashionable. Come on, let me in.'

Mark opened his bedroom door as silently as possible and hurried down to the kitchen. He unbolted the back door and let Jodie in. She was grinning from ear to ear. 'I'm OK,' she said. 'Look, I'm back to normal.'

'But how did you do it?'

'I don't know. I was lying in that cage thinking about everything. It wasn't much fun being a dinosaur, and I was thinking about what was going to happen and Pinkerton-Snark and the TV stuff, and I remembered what you said.'

'Me?'

'You said that if I managed to change into a dinosaur then why didn't I just change back. So I did.'

'But how?'

'Don't ask me – I'm not a magician! All I

can say is that I did it bit by bit. I thought about my fins and I thought about them getting smaller and smaller until they shrank away to nothing – and they did!'

'Wow!'

'Yeah, so when that worked I thought about all the other bits and changed them too.'

Mark suddenly had a thought and he

glanced at his sister's hair. 'It wasn't God then,' he mumbled.

'Wasn't God? What do you mean?'

Mark explained about his prayer, turning a shade red in the process. 'I asked him to give you long, straight hair, preferably blonde.'

'Really?' Jodie looked steadily at her brother. 'I never thought of thinking about long blonde hair.' She chuckled. 'Oh well, never mind. It's good to be back and hey, listen . . .' Jodie frowned. 'Thanks for your help. No, I mean it. You were there looking after me and all that stuff . . . thanks.'

Before Mark could say a word she had whirled round and vanished up the stairs to get changed out of her sack.

Mark followed quietly, trying not to disturb their parents. Jodie changed quickly and came across to Mark's bedroom. She wanted to know how Mum and Dad were.

'They've been going frantic,' said Mark. 'They've been really worried. I don't think Mum's eaten since you, you know . . .'

'I turned into a stegosaurus,' Jodie finished for him. 'Yeah, I know, but I've got something important to do first, something to do with Mr Pinky-Winky. I need to sort him out.'

'*We* need to sort him out,' corrected Mark and Jodie grinned.

'OK, both of us. I've been thinking and I've got a pretty good idea about what we should do . . .'

9 Boo!

Smug, thought Jodie. Smug is by far the best
word to describe Mr Pinkerton-Snark. She
was watching him from the safety of the large
crowd that had gathered at the Animal
Quarantine Hospital to see the dinosaur
revealed. Pinkerton-Snark was helping the
TV crews set up their cameras and lights. He
was beaming from ear to ear and his gold
teeth flashed and twinkled in the hot, bright
glare of the lamps.

Reporters, both TV and press, kept
hurrying across to him to have a word or to
ask questions. Pinkerton-Snark waved them
away imperiously.

'Don't fret, my friends,' he cried. 'All will be
revealed in good time. I shall give you all the
information you could possibly wish for then.'

Jodie's cage had been covered with a large tarpaulin so that it was impossible to see the dinosaur inside. Mr Pinkerton-Snark was hurrying about with an enormous smile, preparing for his grand moment.

Mark gazed out of the office window with his parents, trying to catch a glimpse of his sister, but she was well hidden in the crowd, and it was probably just as well, thought Mark. 'Miss Gatling's out there,' he said, 'and Mrs Farouk. Everybody's come to see Jodie today.'

'She always did like a lot of attention,' sighed Mrs Bolton. 'Oh, I do wish this wasn't happening. I don't want a dinosaur for a daughter. I want our Jodie back, with all her moods and everything.' Mr Bolton slipped a comforting arm round his wife's shoulders.

Outside, a TV interviewer approached Miss Gatling. 'I gather that you were Jodie's headteacher?'

'Indeed, yes.'

'Could I ask you a few questions?' Miss Gatling drew herself as tall as possible and smiled at the camera. 'OK, here we go, cameras roll . . . This is Tamsin Plank reporting live for CBTV News, on the extraordinary case of Jodie Walton – the nine-year-old girl who –'

'Bolton,' corrected Miss Gatling, still maintaining her stiff smile.

'I beg your pardon?'

'Jodie's surname is Bolton, not Walton.'

'Cut!' cried Tamsin and took a deep breath. 'OK, ready, roll . . .' And she began again. 'This is Tamsin Plank for CBTV News, reporting live on the –'

'And she's ten,' added Miss Gatling, with a curt nod to the camera.

'What?'

'Jodie's not nine, she's ten. You said she was nine.'

'Cut!' Tamsin shot daggers at the headteacher. 'Anything else?' she hissed.

'There's no point in feeding the public misinformation,' said Miss Gatling airily.

The glamorous reporter took another deep breath. 'Tamsin Plank for CBTV News, reporting live on the amazing case of Jodie Bolton, the ten-year-old girl who has turned into a dinosaur. I have with me Jodie's headteacher, Miss Gatling.' Tamsin smiled at Miss Gatling. 'What kind of pupil was Jodie?'

'Absolutely charming,' sighed Miss Gatling. 'I never had a cross word with her. She was my star pupil. This is such a terrible tragedy. If only she hadn't turned into a stegosaurus – I was about to make her school captain you know, but I'm afraid animals aren't allowed on the school premises.'

Obviously it was all right for Miss Gatling to feed the public misinformation, even if the TV reporter wasn't allowed to do it. It was a good thing that Mark couldn't hear any of this from inside the office. He would most likely have interrupted himself and spoilt Tamsin Plank's interview for the third time, but Mark's attention was taken up by Pinkerton-Snark, who was making his way to Jodie's cage.

'I think they're ready,' Mark pointed out to his family. 'Come on, let's go outside.'

The Boltons crept out of the office and stood to one side where they could see what was going on without being part of it. The last thing they wanted was to be pestered by the press.

Pinkerton-Snark had taken a position close to Jodie's cage. He stood smiling at the cameras through his half-moon spectacles, clasping the edge of the tarpaulin cover with his pudgy fingers. 'Ladies and gentlemen, I have asked you all here today to bear witness to one of the most extraordinary events in our entire history. Even the youngest babe in arms knows that dinosaurs ruled this earth millions of years ago and then became extinct. A living dinosaur has not been seen on this earth for many hundreds of thousands of years – until now.'

'Mr Shark!' Tamsin Plank was shouting from the bunch of reporters. 'Mr Shark! Are you kidding us? Have you really got a real dinosaur?'

'Snark – Pinkerton-Snark,' bellowed the

specialist. 'Yes, behind this cover there is a real dinosaur – to be precise, a stegosaurus. A week ago, Jodie Bolton was an ordinary nine-year-old girl –'

'Ten!' chorused Tamsin and Miss Gatling.

'And then she changed, overnight. In the morning she found she was a stegosaurus.'

'You're having us on!' cried a newspaper man. 'Nobody can change into a dinosaur. Tell us how it happened.'

'Ladies, gentlemen, please,' said Mr Pinkerton-Snark with an expansive movement of both arms. 'You have my word. Do you think I wish to be made a laughing stock? Of course not! In a few moments you will see for yourselves – and this is no trickery – a real, living stegosaurus, the first new stegosaurus to walk this earth of ours for eons.

'And of course I shall tell you how this came about. I ran hundreds of tests on Jodie

Bolton. I spent many hours trying to locate the source of this mystery. Eventually, I realized that what we had on our hands was no more and no less than a completely new disease – Dinosaur Pox.'

'Dinosaur Pox?' The TV crews crowded forward, bombarding the specialist with questions.

'Can anyone get Dinosaur Pox?'

'Is it infectious?'

'What if the dinosaur escapes? Will we all turn into dinosaurs?'

'Gentlemen!' cried Pinkerton-Snark. 'Calm yourselves, please. You are quite safe. It is very unlikely that anyone else can catch it. And now, if you could just move back a little so that everyone can see, I will remove this tarpaulin and you will behold the stegosaurus for yourself.'

More TV spotlights flashed into life. The

tarpaulin was glaring with intense light as the world's eyes focused on the cage. Pinkerton-Snark moved forward, grasped the cover with both hands and yanked it away.

A hundred flashbulbs popped and a great gasp went up from the crowd. They stared in astonishment, leaning forward to see. And then they began laughing and pointing.

The cage was almost empty, but not quite. Hanging from the ceiling was a huge piece of white card. There was one word written right across it in huge black letters:

FRAUD

Immediately beneath the card, and looking very, very tiny was Mark's little plastic stegosaurus. A small piece of paper was stuck to its jaws, like a speech bubble. It said:

BOO!

Laughter gripped the crowd. They were

clutching themselves. Some were staggering round in convulsions. Others were rolling on the ground. Some clung to each other, with tears rolling down their cheeks.

Pinkerton-Snark had turned the whitest white, staring down at the little toy dinosaur. He dashed round the back and entered the cage himself. He searched  every square centimetre with the desperation of a madman. He bent down, seized Mark's stegosaurus and held it cradled in his hands, staring at it in disbelief. He gazed out at the sea of laughing faces, then he grabbed the bars, rattled them furiously and roared.

'Rraaaaaaaarrrggghhhh!'

It was not like Jodie's roar at all. It wasn't wild and magnificent and spine-tingling. It was a sad and floppy roar, and it died to a whimper as the world's cameras photographed Pinkerton-Snark in his cage. There he was, foaming at everyone as he held the little dinosaur. Jodie and Mark's sign was hanging above his head.

There were some people who weren't laughing. Mr and Mrs Bolton could not believe what they were seeing.

'What's going on?' asked Mr Bolton. 'Where's Jodie?'

One small hand slipped into Mrs Bolton's, and the other hand clutched Mr Bolton's arm. 'I'm here,' said Jodie quietly, and a moment later she was almost crushed to death between her parents as they hugged her silly.

'How? Incredible! I mean . . . What? Where? And the . . .!' Mr Bolton had too many things to say at once, and they jammed in his brain.

'Jodie, Jodie, Jodie,' Mum kept repeating.

'Yes, yes, yes,' laughed Jodie. 'Come on, I want to go home. I want to see what's on the telly.'

'After everything that's happened you want to watch telly? Oh Jodie!' cried Mrs Bolton.

On the way home, Jodie carefully explained how she had managed to change back, and also all about the trick that she and Mark had played on Mr Pinkerton-Snark.

'I never did like him,' muttered Mr Bolton. 'I'm very proud of both of you.'

As soon as they reached the house, Jodie rushed in and switched on the television so that they could all watch the news. There was

Tamsin Plank, flashing her perfect white teeth
at the camera and interviewing onlookers.

'That's Miss Gatling!' cried Jodie, and she
listened with mounting astonishment (and
anger) to her headteacher's comments. 'Star
pupil? School Captain? Ooh, the old –' For
once Jodie was lost for words and Mark filled
the gap.

'Dinosaur!'

'Dinosaur!' everyone chorused, and then

Pinkerton-Snark appeared on the screen, standing under the card sign and gazing hopelessly at Mark's stegosaurus.

'Serves him right,' muttered Mr Bolton, and switched off the television.

'Anyone hungry? I'll make some lunch,' suggested Mum.

'Got any daisies?' asked Jodie.

'You haven't changed a bit,' laughed Mrs Bolton.

But she had changed. Jodie might have seemed the same on the outside, but she was forever different inside. She knew now for certain just how much she meant to everyone in the family. Mark was still a pain, and her parents were still hopeless, but they loved her, even when she was a dinosaur.

When at last it was bedtime, she went and sat in front of her mirror. She didn't grunt at herself this time. She smiled, and she watched how her smile made her nose wrinkle up and she thought it looked quite nice. Shame about the hair – that was still awful.

Jodie looked into the dark, mysterious eyes that gazed back at her from the mirror. They seemed as deep and dark and uncharted as the universe itself, full of hidden promises and strange secrets. Looking into those mirror eyes, Jodie knew that she could go back to being a dinosaur if she wanted – if *she* wanted – at any time.

She smiled at her reflection and whispered, 'Hello, Jodie.' Then she climbed under her duvet and lay there, feeling the warmth of her own bed surround her. If she could be a dinosaur, she thought as she drifted to sleep, why not . . . anything? Maybe things were only just beginning now.